Rise of the Slime Monster

by Liza Charlesworth
illustrated by Zihua Yang

ISBN: 979-8-225-02085-9

Publisher: Tara Welty
Creative Director: Tannaz Fassihi; Designer: Cynthia Ng

1 2 3 4 5 6 7 8 9 10 68 34 33 32 31 30 29 28 27 26 25

Made in Jiaxing City, China. First printing, August 2025.

SCHOLASTIC

Greetings, reader! It is nice to meet you.
My name is Justin Lee and I am nine.
I am an artist and I like to make things.
I like to paint pictures of cool race cars.
I like to craft small animals from clay.

Best of all, I like to make my own
gloppy, sticky, glittery blue slime.
But homemade slime can be spooky.
When I made a batch last week,
I got the biggest surprise of my life.
Turn the page to find out all about it!

OK, let's start at the very beginning. First, I had to gather the stuff I needed to make fresh slime. That took a while. Then I mixed it all up in a big bowl until it got thick and super gloppy. Gee whiz! I was getting good at this.

Even my mother was quite impressed.
“I like the way your slime shines!” she said.
“I’m going to visit Mrs. Jenson next door.
You can play with the slime in the kitchen,
if you promise you will not make a mess.”
“I promise!” I replied with a smile.

Yay! It was time to play with my slime.
Pull and stretch, squish and flatten.
I rolled the slime into a glittering ball
and I tossed it up, up, up. . .OOPSIE!
The slime did not drop back down into
my hand because it got stuck on the light.

Oh, no! Mom would NOT like that a bit.
I had to get that slime ball back quick.
But then, a shocking thing happened.
That sticky blob of blue got bigger
and bigger and bigger and bigger—
until it fell to the floor with a SPLAT!

Oh, my! Things were getting VERY odd.
The ball of slime rolled across the tiles.
Then ZIP, ZAP! It became a new shape.
It had arms, legs, and a long lizard tail.
It also had a glittering blue face. Yikes!
It was a sticky, icky slime monster!

The blue slime monster kept on growing and growing and growing and growing—until it was about the same size as me. Then it opened up its mouth and spoke: "Hello, kid! Do you know what time it is? It's time for the rise of the slime monster!"

After that, it grinned with glee and ran off.
It went up the steps. It went down the steps.
It dashed in and out of each tidy room.
But that was not even the bad part.
The bad part was that the monster left
a trail of gloppy footprints all around!

Dear me! I needed to stop its slime spree!
So, I chased the creature into our den and
what I saw made my haircut stand on end.
The slime monster was sitting at Mom's desk,
writing a silly message on her computer!
Tip, tap, tip, tap. She would not like the note.
And she'd REALLY hate the sticky handprints.

What happened next? The slime monster ran back into the kitchen and grabbed a big jug of chocolate milk from the fridge. Then it jumped up on the table and drank all the milk while doing a jig and burping. I knew right away this was NOT good.

Gadzooks! Our home was now a wreck.
It was up to me to fix things—and quick.
So, I waved my arms and shouted, "STOP!
You are being a rude blue slime monster!
You need to behave! You need to clean
everything up before my mom gets back!"

The slime monster took a look around
and said, “Gee, I see what you mean.
I wasn’t polite. But I can correct this.”
Next it grabbed a rag, mop, and bucket—
Scrub, scrub, scrub! Swish, swish, swish!
The slime monster cleaned up the mess
and, in no time flat, every room gleamed.

“Wow! My home looks perfect!” I exclaimed. “Glad you like it!” replied the slime monster. After that, it shook my hand and said, “Bye! It’s now time to return to where I came from.” ZIP, ZAP! The creature got smaller and smaller—until it took the shape of a gloppy, glittery ball.

The gloppy, glittery ball rolled across the table and right back into the bowl. "Maybe we will meet again," I whispered. I was kind of starting to miss the creature when Mom returned from her visit next door. "I'm glad you kept your promise," she said. "The whole place looks as neat as a pin. I will let you make blue slime anytime!"